GREAT MOUSE DETECTIVE

BOOK 6

Basil and the Big Cheese Cook-Off

CREATED BY *Eve Titus* WRITTEN BY *Cathy Hapka*

ILLUSTRATED BY *David Mottram*

ALADDIN

NEW YORK LONDON TORONTO SYDNEY NEW DELHI

This book is a work of fiction. Any references to historical events, real people, or real places are used fictitiously. Other names, characters, places, and events are products of the author's imagination, and any resemblance to actual events or places or persons, living or dead, is entirely coincidental.

ALADDIN

An imprint of Simon & Schuster Children's Publishing Division
1230 Avenue of the Americas, New York, New York 10020
First Aladdin hardcover edition October 2018
Text copyright © 2018 by Estate of Eve Titus
Illustrations copyright © 2018 by David Mottram
Also available in an Aladdin paperback edition.
All rights reserved, including the right of reproduction in whole or in part in any form.
ALADDIN and related logo are registered trademarks of Simon & Schuster, Inc.
For information about special discounts for bulk purchases, please contact
Simon & Schuster Special Sales at 1-866-506-1949 or business@simonandschuster.com.
The Simon & Schuster Speakers Bureau can bring authors to your live event.
For more information or to book an event contact the Simon & Schuster Speakers Bureau
at 1-866-248-3049 or visit our website at www.simonspeakers.com.
Cover designed by Karin Paprocki
Interior designed by Hilary Zarycky
The text of this book was set in Perpetua.
Manufactured in the United States of America 0918 FFG
2 4 6 8 10 9 7 5 3 1
This book has been cataloged with the Library of Congress.
ISBN 978-1-5344-1860-8 (hc)
ISBN 978-1-5344-1859-2 (pbk)
ISBN 978-1-5344-1861-5 (eBook)

Cast of Characters

BASIL	*English mouse detective*
DR. DAWSON	*his friend and associate*
NIGEL	*young mouse sentry*
ALAIN RONGEUR	*one of mousekind's most celebrated chefs*
PIERRE, HENRI, AND GUSTAVE	*Chef Rongeur's trusted assistant chefs*
CHEF TOPO	*mouse chef from Italy*
CHEF KLEIN	*mouse chef from Germany*
CHEF NEZUMI	*mouse chef from Japan*
THEO	*young Parisian ruffian*
VICTOR	*burly mouse guard*
ADELINE	*female Parisian mouse*
ADELARD	*Adeline's twin brother*
PROFESSOR RATIGAN	*arch villain*
MARCEL	*elderly Parisian gentlemouse*
RAYMOND	*nervous mouse cook*

VARIOUS GUARDS, COOKS, DISHWASHERS, BELLHOPS,
AND OTHERS

Contents

1

SAY CHEESE!

SURELY EVERY MOUSE THE WORLD OVER HAS heard of the International Cheese Cook-Off! Held every year in Paris, it brings together the finest mouse chefs and most discerning lovers of cheese dishes from every corner of the globe.

And of course, every mouse has heard of Basil of Baker Street, the world-famous detective and my dear friend. Basil has solved so many tricky cases that his fame, too, has reached every nook and cranny of the mouse world.

Thus it was no surprise when Basil was called in to save the cook-off from the greatest threat to its existence imaginable and the most evil of plots from the most cunning of criminals—

But allow me to tell you about it from the beginning. . . .

It was the year 1895. Basil and I were at 221B Baker Street, our home as well as that of the world's greatest human detective, Mr. Sherlock Holmes. We were hidden away in a corner of the great man's study. That was where Basil had learned many methods of scientific sleuthing, methods that had served him very well over the years. But he, like Holmes himself, was always eager to learn still more, and so we often sneaked upstairs to eavesdrop.

On that particular evening Basil was listening intently, scribbling notes in shortpaw as the brilliant detective discussed coded messages and handwriting analysis with his dear friend Dr. John H. Watson.

I, however, had quite a different focus. While I had joined Basil on many of his most famous cases, I was at heart still a medical mouse—Dr. David Q. Dawson, at your service—and easily distracted from the in-depth details of detecting. And that night there was plenty to distract me, for Holmes's housekeeper

had set out a platter of fruits and cheeses for the
men, and the odor drifting toward us was heavenly.

"Stilton," I murmured, closing my eyes and
identifying the scents by nose alone. "A creamy
Caboc from Scotland. And, of course, a fine English
Cheddar . . ."

"Hush, Dawson," Basil scolded. "I wish not to
miss a word of this fascinating discussion."

I stayed quiet after that. But later, as the two
of us made our way down to the cellar, where our
mouse town of Holmestead was located, my mind

was still locked on the topic of cheese. "Let's stop at the cheese shop for a nibble," I suggested.

"All right." Basil was nearly always in a fine mood after an evening at Holmes's foot, and tonight was no exception. "I could enjoy a nice bit of Blue Wensleydale myself. . . ."

But halfway to the Holmestead Cheese Emporium, we spied a harried-looking mouse racing toward us. It was a youngster known as Nigel who often stood sentry at the edge of the village.

"Mr. Basil, sir, I've been looking everywhere for you!" he exclaimed. "There's a message for you—from Paris!"

Nigel handed over a note. Basil unfolded it, and I peered over his shoulder, curious. The message was written in a tiny, precise hand, covering the entire sheet of paper, but though my eyesight is good, I could read scarcely a word of it.

"Oh," I said. "It's written in French!"

"Of course." Basil thanked Nigel with a nod, then returned his gaze to me. "Didn't you hear the lad say it comes from Paris?"

As Nigel wandered off, Basil gave his full attention to the note. I waited patiently for him to

translate it for me, knowing him to be fluent in French as well as several other languages. However, he simply refolded the missive and tucked it away in his cape without a word.

"Well?" I prompted him. "What does it say?"

"That can wait," he replied. "Find another doctor to see to your patients for the next few days, Dawson. We depart for Paris first thing in the morning!"

I felt a flash of annoyance. "You expect me to adjust my schedule yet refuse to tell me why?"

Basil merely shrugged. "Not to worry, my friend. All will be revealed in time. For now, let us get some sleep."

With that, he turned and strode off toward home. I clenched my paws, tempted to refuse Basil's orders for once. But even in my fit of temper, my curiosity was piqued, and I knew come morning I would go along with him as usual. . . .

Sure enough, the very next day I found myself scurrying through the streets of London before dawn. The city was quiet, though we knew it was

6

an hour of creeping paws and twitching whiskers and thus kept a careful lookout for cats. Fortunately, we didn't encounter a single feline and soon hitched a lucky ride on a milkman's cart. In that way we safely reached Victoria Station.

"Basil," I said once we'd stowed away on board a train bound for Dover. "When will you clue me in to the reason for our voyage?"

He settled himself in a corner of the luggage shelf where we were hiding behind a large valise. "Right now, of course," he told me, adjusting the deerstalker cap he always wore. "What better way to while away a long journey than with interesting conversation?"

And that, at last, was when I heard the first details of the Case of the Big Cheese Cook-Off.

CITY OF LIGHT

"THAT NOTE WAS SENT BY A DEAR FRIEND FROM university," Basil began.

"Who's that?" I asked, curious at once, for Basil and I had attended Ratcliffe College together in our younger days. "Anyone I know?"

"Yes, of course—Alain Rongeur," Basil replied, and I nodded, remembering the mouse in question very well. But I had little time to reminisce before Basil resumed his tale. "Alain is at the Parisian College of Cooking these days. He is known as one of the finest chefs in all mousedom. He also organizes the International Cheese Cook-Off."

My whiskers twitched. Every mouse knows

of the International Cheese Cook-Off, held every year in Paris. The finest mouse chefs from all over the world travel there to unveil their latest masterpieces, and prizes are awarded in several categories. I'd had no idea an acquaintance of mine was involved in such a stellar enterprise!

"Wonderful," I said.

"Indeed." Basil stroked the fur of his chin thoughtfully. "The cook-off's fame has grown to the point that poor Alain has had some trouble procuring enough Roquefort and Camembert for the proceedings. However, this year a much more serious problem has arisen. Someone is sending threats against the competition!"

"What? Who, pray tell, would do something like that?"

"Alain has no idea," Basil replied. "He has received three separate notes thus far, which he promises to show me upon our arrival. For now he has said only that they assure terrible consequences if the cook-off carries on as usual."

Basil and I had plenty of time to discuss suspects and theories during the rest of the journey. We left the train at Dover, dodging human feet until we found our way up the ramp onto the ferry. It was a magnificent boat, able to make the long trip across the Channel in only one and a half hours—an amazing feat of modern human ingenuity!

After that, it was another long train trip from coastal Calais to Paris. Halfway there I dozed off, waking only when Basil shook me by the shoulder.

"We're here, Dawson," he proclaimed, his voice filled with zeal for the task ahead and no trace of weariness. "Hurry—let's get to work!"

I followed him, yawning at first but soon roused by the sights, sounds, and smells of the City of Light. We exited the busy Gare du Nord train station and looked around.

"How do we reach the College of Cooking?" I wondered, a little overwhelmed by the shouts of the humans and the endless carriages clicking and clacking past in the road. A slender woman hurried by us leading a dog on a leash. The creature's nose twitched; he turned to stare at us with bright, curious eyes and barked, sending me scurrying to the shelter of a cleft in the wall.

But Basil merely laughed. "Ah, Paris!" he exclaimed, throwing his arms wide as if to embrace the city. "A place that loves its dogs, which keeps the cats in check!"

Still chuckling over his own comment, he hurried off. "Wait for me!" I cried, rushing to catch up.

It seemed that Alain had included directions in his note, for Basil knew exactly where to go. We caught a ride on one passing coach and then another, finally finding ourselves in the heart of Paris, steps from the river Seine. Only then did I look up and notice an immense tower rising over the rooftops.

"Look at that!" I said, pointing.

Basil squinted upward and then nodded. "Surely, Dawson, you've heard of the great tower of Monsieur Eiffel?" he said. "It was installed for the Exposition held here a few years ago. Monsieur Eiffel has an apartment at the top, which he uses to conduct meteorological research." He nodded, clearly approving, for Basil was interested in all fields of scientific endeavor. "It's the tallest tower in the known world!" he added.

"Is it?" I stared at the tower until it disappeared from view when Basil and I ducked into a grate in the wall of the cooking school.

Inside, people were rushing about carrying platters and trays, all of which were high overhead and thus out of view. But my nose stayed busy, twitching as one delicious scent after another drifted down to mouse level. Basil and I stayed out of sight, soon finding our way to the cellar beneath the school. Shelves upon shelves stood there, packed with food of every possible variety. I may have drooled a little as I scanned the printing on the packages—TOMATE, PÂTE, CHOCOLAT, and of course, FROMAGE. Even without knowing the French language, I recognized many of those names!

"Basil, Dawson!" A portly mouse dressed in a white jacket appeared from behind a tub of *les petit pois*, better known as peas. "You made it, *mes amis!*"

Our old friend Alain Rongeur looked a bit different than he had when last we'd seen him, but even so, it was suddenly as if we'd all three been transported back to those carefree university days. Several minutes passed in embraces and exclamations.

It was Basil who put an end to that. "So, Alain," he said briskly, stepping back and looking the chef up and down. "Let's have a look at these threatening notes of yours."

"*Oui, oui.*" Alain's face became serious as well. "There is no time to waste, eh? The cook-off is set to commence a mere two days from now. And if you can't crack this conundrum, Basil, I shall have no choice but to cancel!"

3

A TASTE FOR TROUBLE

"YOU WON'T HAVE TO CANCEL—NOT NOW THAT I'm on the case," Basil assured our friend. "But first I must see those notes."

"*Oui*, of course," Alain replied. "Yet you two must be famished after your long journey, *mais non*? Come with me."

He scurried off into the depths of the cellar without pause, for which I was glad. It had been a long journey indeed, and every last crumb of the cheese and bread I'd brought along had been long since gobbled.

"Alain, wait!" Basil called. "The notes, if you please . . ." He trailed off with a frustrated sigh, having little choice but to follow the chef. Hiding a smile, I did the same.

We soon found ourselves in a cozy mouse kitchen built into a nook beneath the humans' staircase, with gleaming copper pots and wooden spoons hanging from the ceiling and delicious odors wafting everywhere. Alain called to several cooks, who quickly seated the three of us at a table topped with a checkered cloth. Seconds later the table was piled with platters and bowls of steaming food—*gougères*, better known as cheese puffs, along with various

quiches, crepes, croissants, and many other dishes that I didn't recognize but couldn't wait to taste.

As we tucked in, Alain pulled several scraps of paper out of his apron pocket. "Voilà! The notes," he said, spreading them on the only bit of tabletop not covered with crockery.

Basil shot a look toward a trio of young mice bustling about the kitchen. "Can we talk freely in front of your workers?"

"Yes." Alain nodded. "While I'm keeping this issue quiet from most of the school and beyond, these three were here when the notes arrived. Please meet Pierre, Henri, and Gustave, my most trusted assistants. They know everything—and have promised complete secrecy."

Gustave, a lean young fellow, heard him and looked over with a wry smile. "We're accustomed to keeping secrets, sir," he said in good English, with only a trace of a French accent. "Every soul in mousedom would love to get a sneak peek at the recipes for the cook-off, which the visiting chefs have provided to ensure we shall have the correct ingredients at paw."

"Yes," Henri, rounder and a little older, added

worriedly. "If indeed there will be a cook-off this year . . ."

Seeming satisfied that the discussion could continue, Basil nodded once to the trio and then turned his attention back to the notes, studying them carefully.

"What do they say?" I asked, for they were of course written in French.

Basil took his time answering, studying first one note, then the next, and finally the third. "Hmm," he said at last, taking a thoughtful bite of quiche. "Dawson, my friend, you really should pick up a bit of French."

"All right." I tried to disguise my impatience. "But as that seems unlikely to happen in the next five minutes, how about a translation?"

Alain picked up the first note. "Dawson, this one reads 'Cancel the cook-off, or suffer the consequences,'" he said. "The others are much the same, with increasing levels of urgency—the second promises the destruction of the cooking school itself if the contest commences, and the third, the peril of all mousedom throughout Paris and beyond."

"Yes." Basil stroked his whiskers, as he often did when deep in thought. "Alain, where were the notes discovered?"

"I found all three in my apron pocket, each arriving one morning after the last," Alain said. "Given the security around the cook-off, it's hard to imagine who could have slipped in overnight to deliver them. But it seems that's exactly what must have happened."

While we talked, Alain's three young assistants had returned to their work. But now Pierre paused beside the table. "Chef Rongeur, sir," he said, "what about the tall stranger that Henri noticed skulking about last week? Could he have left those notes?"

Basil looked up sharply. "A tall stranger?" he said. "I must know more."

Alain whistled to Henri, who was washing dishes nearby. He came over and bowed politely. "I saw him only once, monsieur," he told Basil. "It was in the north alley, near the loading bay. As I said, he was tall, with stooped shoulders, a high, bony forehead, and a rather sly expression."

"Ah." Basil nodded and waved a paw to dismiss the two cooks. "Thank you. That's all I need to know." He turned and smiled at Alain. "The case is more than half-solved, my friend, for I now know the identity of our note-writing rogue."

"You do?" I was so surprised that I nearly choked on my mouthful of baguette. Even for a detective as brilliant as Basil, this was record speed! "Care to fill us in, Basil?"

"Weren't you paying attention, Dawson?" Basil exclaimed. "The culprit is obviously our old nemesis—Ratigan!"

4

AN OLD ENEMY

"RATIGAN?" I EXCLAIMED. "BASIL, SURELY YOU'RE joking—that scoundrel is in prison, thanks to you!"

"Not anymore." Basil looked grim. "The Baker Street Irregulars informed me he escaped a fortnight ago."

"Oh dear," I said with feeling. Professor Padraic Ratigan was a free mouse? That was bad news indeed. Ratigan was the head of the mouse underworld, and the brains and muscle behind much of the trouble throughout mousedom. "But why would Ratigan want to stop the cook-off?" I added. "Despite his countless faults, he loves cheese as much as the next mouse."

Alain cleared his throat. "I suspect I know the answer," he said. "Professor Ratigan contacted me last year offering the use of his goons to provide security for the cook-off in exchange for a share of the proceeds." He shook his head. "Naturally, I refused. Perhaps Monsieur Ratigan holds a grudge?"

"Perhaps." Basil rubbed his slim paws together eagerly. "Our next step is to find him."

"If he's even in Paris, that is," I put in.

"I haven't a doubt he is here." Basil sounded impatient. "Alain, may I interview the rest of your staff?"

"Of course." The chef waved a hand at the kitchen. "Everyone is busy preparing for the cook-off—as you know, it is due to commence in less than two days' time—but I'm sure they can answer a few questions."

With that, Basil set to work, beginning with the three young cooks we'd already met. None but Henri had seen hide nor hair of Ratigan, though Pierre mentioned a younger mouse he'd caught lurking on two separate occasions just outside the school earlier in the week.

"We get a few like that every year, though,"

the cook added with a shrug. "Most likely a local ruffian. They like to make a contest of trying to sniff out the latest new cheese recipes before the cook-off begins."

"Yes," Alain put in, for he was listening to this exchange while stirring a bubbling pot of fondue nearby. "That's why Ratigan thought I might require his dastardly services."

"Indeed." Pen in paw, Basil scribbled a note. "My instinct tells me that Ratigan is, indeed, our culprit. But describe this young ruffian to me—just in case."

Pierre scratched his whiskers. "It was two or three nights ago when I last saw him, sir," he said. "Wasn't much to notice about him, aside from a nick in one ear. Made him look like trouble, like someone who'd been in his share of fights."

"Thank you." After scrawling a few more words, Basil snapped his notepad shut and moved on.

For the next hour, I listened while he interviewed cooks, students, and dishwashers. A few of the mice seemed curious about his purpose, though most were so busy they barely paused to blurt out their responses.

We were talking to a stout dishwasher near a crate of cured meats when Alain reappeared, leading a procession of mice.

"Ah, Basil, Dawson," Alain exclaimed. "It's my honor to introduce you to some of our esteemed visiting chefs—Chef Topo from Italy, Chef Klein who hails from the Black Forest of Germany, and Chef Nezumi from far-off Japan."

All three mice bowed deeply, offering greetings in their own languages. "Has my shipment of Fontina from the Aosta Valley arrived yet, Rongeur?" Chef Topo asked in accented English.

"Let's check, shall we?" Alain gestured for the three visitors to precede him out of the room. As he prepared to follow, he paused beside Basil and me. "Any developments, *mes amis?*" he whispered.

"I'm still working on it," Basil told him. "I remain convinced that Ratigan is the mouse we seek. Now all I need do is prove it—and bring him to justice."

Alain looked concerned. "Please hurry," he said. "Now that the visiting chefs have begun to arrive, it is more urgent than ever to put this trouble to rest before something terrible happens!"

With that, he nodded to us and hurried off.

5

NO TIME TO SPARE

"YOU HEARD THE MOUSE, DAWSON," BASIL SAID AS I stared after Alain and his guests, feeling concerned. "There is no time to waste! Solve this case we must."

"But how?" I followed him across the cellar. "We're no closer to locating Ratigan—if indeed he is our culprit. I must say, Basil, for a mouse so devoted to scientific sleuthing, you appear to be relying quite a bit on hunches and conjecture."

"Not at all, my dear doctor. It's a matter of logic." Basil tapped his head. "Besides, I plan to leave no stone unturned and no theory uninvestigated. It's too late to venture out into the city in search of Ratigan tonight in any case."

"So what shall we do? Just wait and worry?" I wondered.

Basil shook his head. "As part of preparations for the cook-off, Alain has posted guards at every entrance to prevent curious mice from sneaking in. Let's find them and see if they've observed anything suspicious while at their posts."

We set out to do just that. By then the hour was indeed growing late. When we poked our noses outside, Paris had been transformed into a true City of Light, illuminated by gas lamps on the smaller streets and buildings and newfangled electric streetlights elsewhere, giving the entire city a festive look. But we had little time for enjoying the views.

"Of course I've seen mice idling about," said one of the guards, a burly fellow nearly the size of a small rat, in response to Basil's question. "Every mouse in Paris would love a peek inside those kitchens, eh?"

"I suppose that's true," Basil said. "But has anyone aroused your suspicions? Loitered excessively, or seemed ill intentioned?"

"Hmm." The guard rubbed his chin. "I don't think

so; then again, my post is quite public." He waved a paw at the bustling boulevard before us. "You might want to check in with Victor; he's guarding the cellar window in the back corner where no one ever goes. It's close to the kitchens, too."

"Thank you, good sir." Basil bowed briefly, then turned and hurried off. I had to scurry to keep up.

We rounded the edge of the building into an alley. I kept a careful lookout, as it seemed just the type of place where cats might dawdle. But I spotted no ferocious felines; instead, a fast-moving mouse caught my eye.

"Ahoy—you there!" I cried, springing forward to intercept him.

"Dawson, what the dickens are you . . . ? Ahh!" Basil nodded, catching on to my actions—for the mouse whose arm I'd just grabbed had a nick in his ear!

"What's your name, lad?" Basil demanded. Then he said something in French—presumably the same question.

The young mouse glared at us, his dark eyes beady and cool. "I can speak English," he spat out. "And who wants to know?"

Basil drew himself up to his full, and rather impressive, height. "Basil of Baker Street, if you please," he declared.

The young mouse's eyes widened. "*The* Basil of Baker Street?"

"The one and only. Now tell me your name and your reason for being here, or I'll have the authorities ask the next questions."

"Theo." The youngster seemed a bit cowed by Basil's stern manner. "And I was just passing through."

"Passing through—or causing trouble?" I leaned toward him. "Someone saw you lurking about here earlier in the week. Why?"

"No reason. I live near here, that's all." Theo shrugged and shoved his paws into the pockets of his thin, patched trousers. "This here alley's a shortcut." He glanced around, then leaned closer. "But if you want someone suspicious, take a look at *her*."

He nodded past us. I spun around just in time to see a slender young female mouse disappearing around the corner. "What, that young girl?" I said.

"*Oui.* I've seen her here many times." Theo shrugged again. "If you ask me, she seems awfully sneaky."

With that, he rushed away before we could stop him. Basil stood for a moment, looking thoughtful.

"Do you think we should track down that lass?" I asked him.

He glanced the way she'd gone, then shook his head. "We'll never find her with that kind of head start," he declared. "Besides, we should remain focused on our prime suspect, and that remains Ratigan. Now come, Dawson—the hour grows late, and we have much work yet to do."

WAKING UP IN PARIS

AFTER A LATE EVENING OF INTERVIEWS, ALAIN'S assistants showed Basil and me to our rooms. Mine was located near the kitchen and smelled pleasantly of woodsmoke and cheese; within moments I was lost in slumber.

Very early the next morning, I opened my eyes to an impatient knock on the door. It was Basil, of course.

"Rise and shine, Dawson!" he called. "The city awaits!"

I yawned and stretched. "Coming, Basil," I mumbled, already reaching for my clothes.

When I emerged, the cooking school was

already a hive of activity. I sniffed the air, detecting the delectable smell of breakfast. But Basil merely shoved a dry bit of baguette into my paw and called for me to follow.

"We're in Paris, at an actual cooking school, for goodness' sake," I complained as we emerged through the grate on the sidewalk. "Couldn't we at least take ten minutes for a proper breakfast?"

He ignored the question. "Today we search for Ratigan," he announced, striding off down the street. "If he's in Paris, we'll find him."

"Basil!" I shouted. "Look out!"

Basil was always single-minded when in search of the truth, and that morning was no exception. He'd just stepped directly under the nose of a hairy spotted dog tied to a lamp-post! In the blink of an eye, the beast had my dear friend trapped beneath one furry forefoot. "Paws off, you slavering beast!" Basil cried.

I scurried forward, unsure what to do. Before I could decide, something small and gray flashed past. It was another mouse!

"Que c'est laid!" she sang out, dancing around the dog just out of reach. *"Un chien moche!"*

I had no idea what she was saying. But the creature pricked its ears, clearly watching her. The strange mouse let out a whistle, then reached out and poked the dog with the umbrella she was carrying.

That gave me the opening I needed. I dashed forward, heart pounding with fear, and stomped upon the beast's paw. When it yelped and pulled back

in surprise, Basil was able to wiggle free. The dog leaped after us but came up short at the end of its leash, whining with frustration.

"Too bad, my smelly friend," Basil taunted it, seeming unruffled by his close call. "I've been captured by far more fearsome creatures than you and lived to tell the tale!"

Meanwhile, I spotted the mouse who had helped us hurrying off. "Wait!" I called after her. "Thank you, Miss . . . ?"

She turned, eyes darting from me to Basil and back again. "You can call me Adeline," she said in a soft voice with a strong French accent. "And you're welcome. That dog is always causing trouble around here."

Basil bowed to her. "You have my gratitude, mademoiselle," he said. Then he peered at her. "Hang on—haven't I seen you before?"

I gasped, realizing he was right. "That was you last night in the alley!" I cried. "A fellow we were talking to pointed you out to us."

"Indeed." Basil looked alert. "What is your interest in the cooking school, Miss Adeline?"

"The school?" she said, backing away. "Why,

none at all. I don't know what you're talking about. I have to go. . . ."

With that, she disappeared into the hurly-burly of the street. "Shall we go after her, Basil?" I asked. "That mouse Theo thinks she could be up to no good."

"We'll never catch her now." Basil stared after young Adeline. "Besides, I'm dubious about what possible motive a young girl like that could have to cause such trouble. No, we can find her later if my current theory is disproven."

"I've been considering motives," I said as I fell into step beside him, skirting well out of the tied dog's way as we passed. "I know you believe Ratigan is out for revenge. But why would he go about it like this—sending secret notes and such? It doesn't really seem like him, does it?"

"Perhaps not," Basil said. "But Ratigan is a master criminal with many tricks up his felonious sleeves. In any case, we can ask his motives once we find him—so let's get on with it!"

A BREAK IN
THE CASE

BASIL AND I SPENT THE NEXT SEVERAL HOURS scouring Paris for any news of Ratigan. We interviewed countless mice, most of whom had no idea of the famous criminal's whereabouts. But a few claimed to have seen a mouse matching Ratigan's description lurking around Paris over the past week. And finally, an elderly mouse named Marcel told us what we needed to know.

"I know exactly where that villain is staying," he said in a quavering but steadfast voice. "Saw him entering myself."

"Pray tell us where, good sir," Basil said.

The old mouse cocked his head. "You sure you

want to find him?" he demanded. "That one is trouble, that's all he is."

"We know," I said. "That's why we want to find him. Basil has captured Ratigan more often than any other detective or police officer in the world!"

Marcel looked suitably impressed at that. "Is this the famous Basil of Baker Street? I'd know you by your sterling reputation, of course! The most masterful detective in mousedom. Well then, *s'il vous plaît*, be on your way to capture him yet again!" he exclaimed. "He's staying at the Opera de Paris—the most expensive building in the city, and according to some, the most magnificent."

"Leave it to Ratigan to stay in such a place," I said. "Where is this wondrous building, sir?"

The old gentlemouse gave us directions, and with that we were off again. When we reached the Opera, we saw that it was indeed an impressive building—and a large one.

"How are we to find one mouse in all of that?" I wondered.

As usual, Basil was filled with confidence. He waited until no humans were nearby and then scurried right in through the front door, which stood open to capture the breeze. I followed him into a grand entryway with marble and gold everywhere. The place was enormous!

"I think every mouse in the world could fit in here, with room for more!" I exclaimed, tipping my head back to look up, up, up at the ornate ceiling.

For his part, Basil hardly seemed to notice the impressive surroundings. "There!" he said, pointing to a baseboard near the staircase.

I followed his gaze and saw what his sharp eyes had spotted—a small mousehole nearly hidden in shadow. We dashed through it and followed a long, twisting corridor until we found ourselves in a busy and most elegant mouse hotel tucked between the walls.

A bellhop spotted us and hurried over. "How may I be of service, monsieurs?" he asked with a deep bow. "We're nearly fully booked—everyone is already arriving for the International Cheese Cook-Off, you see. But I might be able to find a couple more rooms."

"No need for that, my good mouse," Basil said. "We seek only information. Do you have a guest staying here by the name of Professor Ratigan?"

"Ratigan?" The bellhop looked alarmed. "*Mon Dieu*, I certainly hope not! That mouse is infamous the world over for his terrible crimes!"

"Yes, that's why we're looking for him," I said. "We're afraid he's trying to tamper with the Cheese Cook-Off."

"Oh dear!" The bellhop looked more horrified than ever. "Well, what does this Ratigan look like?"

As Basil described Ratigan, I watched the comings and goings in the hotel lobby. Suddenly I spied a tall mouse hurrying up the staircase. He was disguised in a long cape, but I would recognize that stooped figure anywhere!

"There he is!" I whispered urgently, grabbing Basil by the sleeve. "Ratigan—he's headed upstairs."

Luckily the scoundrel hadn't noticed us. We were able to follow him upstairs, where he disappeared into a room.

"Now what?" I wondered. "We can't exactly knock on the door and ask him if he sent those notes, can we?"

Basil paid no attention to me. He was fiddling in the voluminous pockets of his coat. Finally he pulled out a small folding mirror.

"What are you going to do with that?" I asked.

"Watch and see, my dear doctor," Basil said. Without further explanation, he crouched down and slid the mirror partway beneath the door, facing upward. In that way, we could see in the reflective surface a little bit of what was happening in the room!

"What a clever trick!" I exclaimed softly, watching as the slightly blurry figure of Ratigan sat at a desk scribbling busily in some kind of journal or notebook.

But my voice must have been louder than intended, for Ratigan suddenly looked sharply in our direction.

"Dawson, hush!" Basil hissed. "Oh, never mind—run!"

NEW PLANS AND
NEW PROBLEMS

WE ESCAPED WITHOUT BEING SEEN AND RETURNED to the cooking school, which was quite close by. There we found Alain in the kitchen overseeing the creation of a variety of dishes, all of them smelling heavenly. As soon as he saw us enter, the chef immediately chased away all the workers except for his three trusted assistants: Pierre, Henri, and Gustave.

"But the special cheese soufflé—it's nearly ready," protested an anxious-looking cook with crooked whiskers. "You'll need to taste it before we can proceed with the full recipe, Chef."

"That can wait a moment, Raymond. Now go."

Alain shooed the junior cook out of the room.

At the same time, Pierre was waving us to our usual spots at the chef's table, while Gustave and Henri provided us with steaming cups of strong coffee.

"There," Alain said as the door shut behind the last of the others. "Now—what have you found? Am I going to have to cancel the cook-off?"

"Not on your life," Basil said. "We've just returned from the Opera de Paris. . . ."

With my help, he went on to tell Alain all that had happened.

"So Ratigan is indeed in Paris, eh?" the chef said after we'd finished our tale. "And you think he sent those notes, Basil? If so, how shall we prove it?"

"I've already thought about that," Basil said. "And you're right—though I'm sure Ratigan is behind those threats, we will indeed need proof."

"But how?" I asked.

"Elementary, my dear Dawson." Basil smiled. "We need to get our paws on a pawwriting sample."

"A pawwriting sample?" I echoed. "Why?"

"To compare to those notes, of course! If Ratigan is behind the threats, I'm quite sure he wrote those notes himself. He's a perfectionist and prefers always to be in control—he would never leave such an important task to an underling."

"All right," Alain said. "But how in the name of all cheese do you intend to put your paws on a sample of Ratigan's writing?"

"We saw him just now scribbling notes in a book," I told him.

"Yes," Basil said. "So all we need to do is sneak into Ratigan's room and steal a page from that book."

"But how?" I asked. "You and I can't risk it—if he spies us lurking about, he'll recognize us and surely guess that we're onto him. Then we might never figure out what he's up to in time to stop it!"

Basil remained unruffled. "That's why we'll have to get someone else to do it. Perhaps one of your staff, Alain?"

Alain's three assistants had been working nearby as usual. Pierre immediately turned toward us. "I will volunteer if you can spare me, Chef Rongeur," he said. "I know what Ratigan looks like, and I'm familiar with that hotel—my aunt works there. She can help sneak me in if necessary."

"That's a good lad," Basil said. "Thank you, monsieur."

Pierre bowed in response. "I'm happy to help if it means saving the cook-off," he said. Then he glanced at Alain. "Chef?"

Alain looked worried but nodded shortly. "As long as you know what you're in for, lad," he said. "Ratigan is a dangerous character."

"I know," Pierre said. "I'll be careful."

"Good. Be quick, too. We can't spare you for long." With that, Alain gave him a clap on the shoulder and sent him on his way.

"There, that should take care of things." Basil leaned back in his chair and sipped his coffee. "In the meantime, perhaps we—"

Before he could finish, the crooked-whiskered cook, Raymond, rushed back in. "Chef Rongeur, sir!" he cried. "Something terrible has happened— someone has stolen the tasting sample of your signature soufflé!"

9

THE DISAPPEARING SOUFFLÉ

"WHAT?" ALAIN CRIED, JUMPING TO HIS FEET. "HOW could that be?"

"I thought you were currently preparing it for the chef to taste," Basil said to the junior cook.

"That's right, monsieur." Raymond looked miserable. "I stepped away for only a moment to check on the ratatouille. When I returned, the soufflé was gone!"

"Well, it can't have gone far." Basil strode toward the door. "Show me where you last saw it, if you please."

Alain looked concerned. "Certainly. But it's almost as if this cook-off is cursed," he muttered.

"Perhaps I should go ahead and cancel after all."

I wasn't sure how to respond to that, so I remained mum. By then we'd all reached a prep area around the corner from the main kitchen near the back of the building. There on a table lay a plate—empty of all but a few crumbs.

Several other cooks had gathered around, chattering excitedly about what had happened. Then one of them pointed to some paw prints leading to a window standing slightly ajar. "Look!" he cried. "Perhaps the soufflé thief escaped that way!"

Basil and I leaped into action, shimmying out through the window. When we dropped to the ground outside, we nearly landed on another mouse—a familiar one. For there in the back alley sat Theo, the young mouse with the nicked ear. And in his paw was a half-eaten cheese soufflé!

"It was you!" I cried.

I grabbed the youngster by the shoulder. "All right, sir," I said sternly. "Would you care to explain this thievery? Because I'm starting to think you may be up to no good—in more ways than one. We can see that you stole the soufflé—are you trying to shut down the cook-off as well?"

"What?" Theo's eyes widened. "Oh, no, monsieur! I would never do such a thing. I love the cook-off! That's why I, uh . . ." His voice trailed off, and his eyes dropped to the ground.

"What is it, lad?" I asked. "Tell us the truth, if you know what's good for you."

"The truth?" Theo glanced at me, then at Basil. "The truth is . . . I love food!" He held up the half-eaten soufflé. "I live for fine cuisine and cookery. It's all I think about! That's why I'm always here trying to catch a look, a sniff . . ." He licked his snout, glancing again at the soufflé. "A taste."

Basil and I traded a surprised look, for this was not at all what we'd expected to hear. "Oh, I see," Basil murmured.

"It's true—ask anyone who knows me," Theo continued. "As soon as I'm old enough I intend to apply to work at the cooking school. Chef Rongeur is my hero!"

I chuckled. "He'll be glad to hear it," I said.

"But come with us, young mouse—you'll have to confess to your hero yourself. He's wondering what became of his soufflé."

We started to herd him toward the window. But he stopped and pointed. "If it's a troublemaker you're after, there she is!" he exclaimed.

I turned and saw Adeline; she had just rounded the corner and looked startled to see us. "Stop right there!" Basil barked out.

She obeyed. I looked to see what Theo would say next—but he'd disappeared! I supposed the thought of facing his hero with what he'd done was too much for his nerves.

"Or maybe he just sneaked off to finish that soufflé," I murmured with a smile.

By the time I caught up to Basil, he was questioning the young female mouse. "I promise you, monsieur, I'm not up to any trouble!" she was exclaiming. "I was just visiting my—my twin brother. He works in the kitchen."

"Does he?" Basil sounded surprised. "Well, whyever didn't you tell us before? How can we find this brother of yours? And what is his name?"

"His name?" She blinked twice, sounding

nervous—and no wonder! Basil could be an impos-
ing figure indeed. "His name is Ad—Adelard. He
looks much like me—but male, of course. There
are no female mice allowed to work in the cooking
school."

"All right. If your brother will vouch for you,
and Alain has hired him, I suppose that's good
enough for me." Basil eyed Adeline with lingering
suspicion. "Good day, mademoiselle."

We hurried back inside, intending to seek out Adeline's brother. But we were distracted by Alain rushing to meet us. "Pierre has already returned with your writing sample," the chef said, waving a sheet of paper before us. "One doesn't have to be an expert nor a super sleuth to see the truth—the writing on those threatening notes looks nothing like it at all!"

10
RUNNING OUT
OF SUSPECTS?

"NOW WHAT?" I ASKED AS BASIL AND I STUDIED THE notes and the sample. As Alain had already told us, they were clearly penned by two totally different paws. "Will the cook-off have to be canceled after all? Ratigan was our only suspect!"

"On the contrary, Dawson." Basil sounded undaunted. "He was our best suspect, perhaps, as he so often seems to be. But he's far from the only one."

"Are you thinking of young Theo?" I asked. "I thought we'd determined he was guilty only of a taste for fine cuisine."

"We've determined nothing of the sort," Basil

said. "Being guilty of one thing is rarely an alibi for a second crime. But Theo is not the mouse I'm thinking of. I'd like to locate Adeline's twin brother and ask him a few questions about his sister."

I looked around for Alain, who had hurried off to check on something or other. "Shall we ask Alain where we might find this Adelard fellow?"

"Let's not bother," Basil said. "It will be better to question him without his boss there to make him nervous."

I nodded at the detective's wisdom and we set out, asking after Adelard. Nobody seemed to know him, which struck me as odd.

"Perhaps he's one of Chef Rongeur's temporary workers," Assistant Chef Gustave suggested when we asked him. "I don't remember all their names. He hires them for the cook-off, since we're so busy then."

"I see." Basil nodded. "Well, this Adelard is said to be slim of face, with large eyes and . . ."

"There!" I broke in, pointing at a mouse hurrying past with a tray of dirty dishes. "That must be him. He looks uncannily like his sister!"

The mouse in question indeed bore a strong

resemblance to Adeline—except, of course, that he was dressed in a young male's trousers, shoes, and cap along with a crisp white apron.

"Good eye, Dawson," Basil said. "Come—let's talk to the lad."

"Yes, Adeline is my sister," Adelard told us in a gruff, raspy voice once we'd started questioning him. "Is she all right?"

"Oh, yes, don't worry," I said. "We're just wondering why she always seems to be hanging around here."

"She's a good girl, never causes any trouble at all," Adelard said. "She lives nearby and sometimes comes to walk me home from work, that's all."

"Every mouse we talk to seems to live near here," I muttered. Then again, I supposed that wasn't surprising—in a bustling city like Paris, lots of mice live near everywhere!

"Would your sister have any reason to threaten the cook-off?" Basil asked.

Adelard's eyes widened. "Oh, no, monsieur, not at all!" he exclaimed. "She loves the cook-off as much as anymouse! Besides, she would never want to hurt my chances of becoming a fine chef myself one day—it's my life's fondest dream." He smiled slightly, looking a bit wistful.

"I see. Thank you, lad." Basil turned and hurried away.

I followed, feeling concerned—especially when I noticed a clock hanging near the cellar stairs. *Ticktock, ticktock* . . . It seemed to be marking down the moments until the International Cheese Cook-Off.

"What now?" I asked Basil. "We seem to have run out of suspects."

"Indeed it seems that way, my friend," Basil replied. "If our culprit is not Ratigan, nor Theo, nor Adeline . . ." He narrowed his eyes and glanced around the busy cooking school. "Well, then, it could be just about anyone!"

11

SPYING A
VILLAIN

I WAS ALARMED TO HEAR BASIL SOUND SO FAR FROM solving the case—especially with the cook-off due to begin bright and early the very next morning!

"Whatever shall we do?" I exclaimed. "We have to figure out who sent those notes—and what the threats might mean!"

Basil nodded, tapping his chin. "It seems odd that someone could have sneaked in three nights in a row to leave them," he mused. "Let's interview the guards again. If they can assure us that they never left their posts, it might point to an inside job."

"What—you mean someone from the cooking

school did it?" I exclaimed. "But who—and why?"

"First things first, Dawson." Basil strode off.

The guard named Victor was once again at his post just outside the cellar window in the back alley. Seeing him there suddenly gave me the feeling that something wasn't right about the scene. But it was only when Basil spoke that I realized why—and that the dazzling detective had already noticed the very same thing.

"A young mouse climbed in and out of this window to steal a soufflé from the kitchen earlier today," Basil said with no preamble. "How did he do that when you're supposed to be on guard here?"

Victor opened his mouth, then shut it again, looking startled. "Er . . . No English?" he tried with an overly dramatic French accent.

Basil crossed his arms over his chest. "As I'm sure you recall, we've already spoken on an earlier occasion, sir. I know you speak fine English. Now please answer my question."

Victor's shoulders slumped, and he looked sheepish. "Sorry, sir," he said. "Theo is my nephew. I—er—might have looked the other way when he sneaked in to get a look at the cookery. He's very interested in such things, you see—been that way his whole life."

"That's what seemed wrong," I murmured to myself. "Victor was nowhere in sight when we found Theo out here earlier."

"And what about others?" Basil asked the guard. "Did you look the other way for any other mouse to sneak inside?"

"Of course not!" The guard drew himself to his full height. "Only my nephew was allowed to slip past me. I would never endanger the school or the cook-off by letting any other mouse by!"

"He sounds sincere," I whispered to Basil.

My friend seemed inclined to agree. He thanked Victor and then hurried off around the corner. "At least we've solved one mystery," he told me once we were out of earshot and strolling toward the front of the building. "But now we must—hush!"

I grunted with surprise as he suddenly slammed me against the wall, pressing himself into a nook beside me. "What is it?" I hissed. "A cat?"

He shushed me again, then peered carefully

out of our hiding place. I did the same—and my eyes widened when I saw who was standing just a few paces away. It was Ratigan! He was halfway between our hiding spot and the street, with three tough-looking mice beside him. All four of them were staring intently at the side of the cooking school building.

After a moment, Ratigan and his goons hurried off and disappeared into the street. Only then did Basil and I creep forward to see what they had been looking at with such interest.

"It's a loading dock of some sort," I said, staring

at a crate marked JARLSBERG OST, which reminded me that it was well past lunchtime. "Could Ratigan have sneaked in this way when the humans opened the doors?"

"Perhaps, but why?" Basil said. "Alain's kitchen is all the way across the cellar from here—Ratigan would be risking almost certain discovery, especially if he tried to sneak in three nights in a row. I should have realized as much when that assistant chef mentioned where he'd spotted him lurking about previously." He shook his head. "But that's all beside the point. Ratigan didn't write those notes—I'm as sure of it as I am my own name."

At that moment Alain appeared from inside with several of his assistants. The junior cooks set out extracting cheese from the crates and rushing off with it, but Alain spotted us and came over.

"Have you solved it, Basil?" he asked anxiously. "If I'm to cancel the cook-off, I need to do it soon—there are only hours to spare!"

"Not just yet," Basil said. "But trust me, old friend—I'm on the verge of cracking the case."

Alain's expression turned to one of relief. I glanced at Basil, worried now myself. As far as I knew, we were no closer to solving the mystery than we'd ever been. And seeing Ratigan here at the school wasn't making my mind rest any easier about the situation.

Would Basil's confidence lead to a solution—or to disaster?

12
DESPERATE DETECTING

OVER THE COURSE OF THE NEXT HOUR OR MORE, Basil and I interviewed every guard on duty outside the school. All claimed to have kept their posts completely secure over the past week.

When we completed our circle, we found ourselves walking toward that rear cellar window yet again. And there was Theo, looking miserable as his uncle Victor scolded him roundly.

"I'm sorry," the young mouse told us when we approached. "Please don't hold my escapades against my uncle."

"Hmm." Basil tapped his chin. "Perhaps there's a way you can make it up to us, lad."

"Anything!" Young Theo brightened instantly. "I'll do anything to help."

"Then find us that female mouse you pointed out earlier, if you please," Basil said. "I'd like to ask her a few questions."

"Er, of course," Theo said. "I'll go find her right now."

As he scurried off, Basil climbed back inside. I followed. "Why do you wish to speak to Adeline?" I asked him.

"Her brother might have sneaked her in," Basil said. "In fact, she could have left the notes."

"But why?" I said. "Adelard told us she loves the cook-off—why would she try to force Alain to cancel it?"

"Precisely why this is a mystery, Dawson." Basil looked thoughtful. "But if it indeed turns out that nobody sneaked in to leave those messages, that leaves only the staff as suspects. Let's question them again—beginning with Alain's assistants. After all, the three of them were the only ones who knew about those nefarious notes. . . ."

I had trouble believing that Pierre, Henri, or Gustave could want to shut down the cook-off.

Then again, Basil had revealed other seemingly earnest and honest mice to have hearts full of deceit and crime, and so I was willing to go along with his plan.

We'd questioned those three and a dozen more besides when Theo finally returned, breathless and frowning. "I've searched and scoured the city!" he exclaimed. "Adeline is nowhere to be found! Her neighbor says he's seen neither whisker nor hair of her since yesterday."

"That seems rather suspicious," I said. "If she's so fond of the cook-off, wouldn't she stick around to enjoy it?"

"An excellent question, Dawson," Basil replied. "And I do have a hunch as to the answer. But first, let's find her brother and see if he can confirm my suspicions."

We went in search of Adelard. Theo trailed after us, his eyes wide and interested as we passed busy mouse cooks going about their work. "Careful, lad," I told him with a smile. "You're starting to drool."

Theo wiped his snout quickly, then smiled sheepishly as he realized I was joking. "This is incredible," he said, watching as a chef grated fresh Parmesan over a delicious-looking casserole. "I feared I might never see the inside of this magnificent place!" He shot me a sidelong glance. "Legally, anyhow."

I smiled and turned away to ask a passing dishwasher if he'd seen Adelard. "Who?" he said. "Oh, you mean the new guy. He's over that way."

We followed his directions and finally located Adelard, who was sweeping up in a distant corner of the cellar. "My sister?" he said. "Er, she has left Paris to visit relatives in, uh, Scotland. I don't know when she'll be back."

I didn't understand why the young mouse seemed so excessively nervous. I was also perplexed as to why Adeline would depart so suddenly, as neither she nor her brother had given any hints of such a move. "Scotland?" I echoed. "But why now, just before the cook-off?"

Just then a mouse called for help carrying some heavy bags of mozzarella, and Adelard used that as an excuse to scurry off posthaste.

Basil watched him withdraw with narrowed eyes. "Hmm, perhaps my hunch was incorrect for once. Because something's amiss here," he said. "I can tell when a mouse is lying, and Adelard was definitely lying just now. But why?"

I gasped as the answer hit me. "What if it's him?" I exclaimed. "You said someone on the inside could have left those threatening notes. Maybe it was Adelard—and perhaps his sister is in on the plot as well!"

"I suppose you could be correct, Dawson," Basil said slowly, though he seemed troubled. "Let's have Alain collar the scoundrel and question him

further." Basil made a move to stride off in the direction the young mouse had gone.

But Theo, whose very presence I'd nearly forgotten about, leaped forward and stopped him by clutching his sleeve. "No, don't do that, monsieur," he cried. "Please! I—I can't do this any longer. That mouse had nothing to do with it—or his sister, either."

"How do you know?" I demanded.

Theo took a breath so deep it made his whiskers quiver. "Because it was me!" he confessed miserably. "I did it—I'm the one who left those threatening notes!"

13

A CONFOUNDING CONFESSION

"I KNEW IT!" BASIL EXCLAIMED, WHILE I GASPED IN surprise.

"Yes, it was me." Young Theo's whiskers drooped as he stared at the floor. "I know it was wrong. But I—I didn't want anyone hurt!"

"Hurt? How do you mean?" I asked.

He hesitated, fear flashing through his dark eyes. But then he took another deep breath. "I have to tell you," he said, seeming to speak more to himself than to us. "I have to!"

"Tell us what?" By now I was thoroughly confused.

Basil said nothing. He merely waited, watching the young mouse closely.

"I've done things I'm not proud of," Theo said after a moment. "Terrible things. There's not much work in these parts for a poor, uneducated young mouse like me. So, when a tough-looking fellow offered my friends and me a week's worth of cheese to help smuggle some bags into Paris, well . . ."

"What tough-looking fellow?" I asked, more perplexed than ever. What did any of this have to do with the cook-off?

"Ratigan." Basil spat out the name as if it tasted foul. "It was he, was it not? Just as I suspected ever since the moment we spied him at that loading dock."

"Yes," Theo said with a shudder. "But I didn't realize it was him at first. I also didn't realize what the bags were for. When I found out, I knew I had to do something."

"And what were they for?" I asked.

"Poison." Theo frowned, his eyes flashing with fury. "The bags were filled with poison powder, tasteless and nearly invisible to the eye when sprinkled over food. That scoundrel planned to poison all the cheese used in the cook-off!"

"No!" I blurted out, horrified at the very thought.

"Indeed!" Basil said at the same time. "I had already formed a hypothesis that this is why Ratigan has been lurking around the loading bay. He meant to taint the cheese when it came through there. That way he had no need to sneak into the cooking school."

"I was afraid to tell anyone once I realized the ruthless Ratigan was behind it." Theo shuddered again. "Who knows what he'd do to me if he found out? So instead, as much as I hated the thought, I tried to stop the cook-off so no mouse would be hurt. I did it in the only way I could come up with—by convincing my uncle to let me sneak in so I could leave those notes." He paused. "Uncle Victor didn't know what I was doing, though—he just thought I wanted a look at the kitchens." He glanced around. "Which I did, actually," he added softly.

Basil hardly seemed to hear the last part of the youngster's confession. "The cheese is already coming in for the cook-off," he said. "What if . . . ?"

"Stop!" I yelled, turning and rushing through the basement, waving my paws above my head. "Everyone, please listen—don't eat any of the cheese!"

A short while later, Alain had been notified and had repeated my command in French. All the cheese that had already come into the school had been gathered up and was being checked for poison. Meanwhile Basil and I still had one errand left to do. We headed back out into the city in search of Ratigan.

When we arrived at the Opera de Paris, we

discovered that our task would be easier than we might have hoped for, as Ratigan was loitering in the lobby with the same goons we'd seen earlier. "Halt, *arrêt!*" Basil shouted, pointing. "Someone arrest that mouse!"

The villain froze. "Basil of Baker Street," he growled. "What are you doing here?"

"Stopping you from another dastardly deed. We know all about your plot against the cook-off, Ratigan." Basil waved to some Parisian policemice who'd just come in. "Quickly—arrest him!"

"*Au revoir* for now, Basil." With that, Ratigan spun and fled out the back door—with Basil, myself, and the police hot on his trail.

Unfortunately, he lost us near the Gare de Lyon train station. By the time a helpful mouse lady told us she'd seen him scurrying aboard a train, it had departed—for far-off Venice, Italy.

"At least he won't be able to sneak back and try to carry out his plot," Basil said, studying the posted timetable. "It's a direct train. By the time he could catch another back to Paris, the cook-off will be but crumbs."

We told the police the entire tale, then returned

to the cooking school to inform Alain. We tracked him down in the kitchen, where I was surprised to see him glaring at young Adelard.

"I demand to know who you are and what you're doing here!" he was saying when we walked in.

14

ONE LAST MYSTERY

"WHAT'S GOING ON HERE?" I ASKED, HURRYING FOR-ward. "What has Adelard done?"

"You know this mouse?" Alain spun to face me and Basil. "Because I've never seen him before in my life!"

"But you hired him," I said, confused.

Alain shook his head. "I told you, I have never before laid eyes on him. I just caught him sneaking a taste of one of my special pastries for the cook-off!"

My ears perked up at that. "Do you mean the cook-off is still on?"

"I don't know." Alain glanced at Basil. "Is it?"

"Indeed, it is." Basil nodded with great cer-
tainty. "Ratigan can't possibly make it back to Paris
in time to interfere—even if the police hadn't
agreed to provide extra security for the cook-off
this year, just in case." He paused. "That is, if the
cheese hasn't all been poisoned already?"

"It has not—we've checked and had to dis-
card only one crate of Camembert." Alain looked
relieved. Then he noticed Adelard trying to sneak
away, and his expression darkened again. "But it
seems there are still mice about trying to cause
trouble, this time by sneaking in and pretending
to work here," he added. "I'm losing patience, lad.
Identify yourself and your purpose here!"

Adelard frowned—then whipped off his cap.
Or, rather, *her* cap—for I immediately recognized
the young mouse as none other than Adeline!

"You!" Basil cried. "Of course. Why didn't I see
it before? I knew there was something suspicious
about you two but wasn't quite able to work out
exactly what. But now I see—there was never a
brother, was there? It was you all along!"

I chuckled. "It seems you're not the only master of disguise around here, Basil."

He ignored me. "But why?" he demanded. "What made you disguise yourself as a boy?"

"Because I love to cook—and I'm good at it." Adeline jutted out her whiskers defiantly. "This was the only way I could think of that I might be able to enter the cook-off."

"A female chef?" Alain looked scandalized. "I've never heard of such a thing! It simply isn't done!"

But Basil was thoughtful. "Perhaps not," he said. "But times are changing, old friend. Why, back in

London human women are working in libraries, in hospitals—even as lawyers! Why should we mice be left behind? Why *not* a female chef?"

"Basil!" I was a little shocked to hear him say such things, him being in many ways such an old-fashioned mouse. "Do you really think so?"

"Of course." He waved a paw. "Consider Mrs. Dunlop back home, who works just as hard as her husband running the Holmestead Bakery. Alain, my old friend, I really think you should give this lass a chance."

Alain gasped. "You do?"

"Of course. I am eager to taste your entry myself," Basil told Adeline with a smile.

Alain didn't speak for a moment. Finally, he sighed and shrugged. "Is this really what you want, Basil?" he said. "I certainly owe you a favor for stopping Ratigan. If you really think I should let her cook . . ."

"I do," Basil assured him.

Alain nodded. "Then let it be so." He shook a paw in Adeline's face. "But no more lying, you hear me?"

"Oh, thank you!" Adeline looked so excited,

she wasn't sure what to do. Then she let out a squeak. "Oh dear, the contest is tomorrow! I'd better start my dough rising *tout de suite*. . . ."

I chuckled as she raced away, muttering about flour and sugar and various other ingredients. "That's another case closed, eh, Basil?" I commented.

Alain clapped us both on the shoulder. "Perhaps. But I've another most difficult case for you."

"You do?" I said.

Our old friend nodded. "There's a lot to do before tomorrow," he said. "Especially since we have to bring in more cheese to replace that poisoned Camembert. It's all paws on deck between now and sunrise tomorrow—and that means I'll need to put you two to work as well. The next case you'll need to tackle is a heavy case of cheese!"

THE INTERNATIONAL CHEESE COOK-OFF

THE INTERNATIONAL CHEESE COOK-OFF WAS A resounding success. Mice poured into the school from all over Paris and beyond. Many were there to enter, and many more to taste. From dawn until well after dusk, the judges were kept busy arguing over the merits of this quiche versus that tart, one creamy fondue versus another nearly as tasty— along with countless other delicious recipes too numerous to mention.

As for Basil and me, we ate so much we could hardly move! Best of all was getting the chance to taste the dishes of various mice we'd met on our visit to Paris. Alain's assistant chef Henri produced a stupendous truffade, and Gustave baked a goat cheese profiterole that was lighter than air. The visitor from Italy, Chef Topo, made the most luscious ricotta cannelloni I could imagine, and there were foods provided by the many other foreign chefs from faraway lands—Switzerland, Norway, Morocco, and beyond.

But two entries were even more special than the others, at least to Basil and me. One belonged to Adeline, who concocted a croquembouche—a tower of pastry higher than her head—that made every visitor *ooh* and *aah* when they merely glimpsed it. And it tasted just as good as it looked!

The second special entry belonged to none other than Theo! When Alain heard about the young mouse's assistance in bringing Ratigan to justice—or at least chasing him out of Paris—he insisted on letting the lad enter as well. Basil and I were proud to taste the result, a savory French onion soup oozing with melted Gruyère.

"I daresay, Dawson," Basil declared as we awaited the judges' final rulings. "This just might be the tastiest case we've yet solved."

"I think you're right." I stifled a soft burp. "We

might wish to investigate the International Cheese Cook-Off every year, eh?"

Basil chuckled. "Better safe than sorry, my friend."

We were both still laughing when Alain called for attention. "The results are in," he announced, waving the sheaf of papers he'd just been handed by the panel of judges. "And here they are. . . ."

He read off a list of the chefs who had won each of various categories—Best New Dish, Cheesiest Dish, Best Foreign Dish, and so on. We clapped politely for each name, adding some polite *whoop*s when Henri won the Best Rustic Dish category.

Finally Alain paused. "And now, for the top prize of the day—Best Overall Dish," he said. He glanced at the paper again and his eyes widened. "Oh, I say! The winner is—Mademoiselle Adeline Chaumes!"

A roar of surprise went up from the crowd. A few of the chefs looked disapproving when they realized they'd been bested by a girl.

But what matters most to mouse chefs is food—and most in the room had to admit that Adeline's dish had indeed been outstanding. Chef Klein, the visiting chef from Germany, was the first to congratulate her.

"Well done, *fräulein*," he said. "I look forward to tasting whatever dish you make next year."

"N-next year?" Adeline smiled uncertainly.

"Of course." Alain came over to clap her on the back. "You must defend your title, after all!" He winked and smiled. "A chef is only as good as his—or her—last dish, eh?"

"And a detective is only as good as his last case," Basil said. "Come, Dawson—it's time to return to London and alert the authorities at Mouseland Yard that Ratigan is running rampant again. Because I have a feeling we'll be seeing him sooner or later."

"I hope it's later," I said. "And we can leave soon, Basil. But first one more taste of that cheese profiterole. Look, there's one left for you as well. *Bon appétit!*"